When Will It Snow?

When Will It Snow?

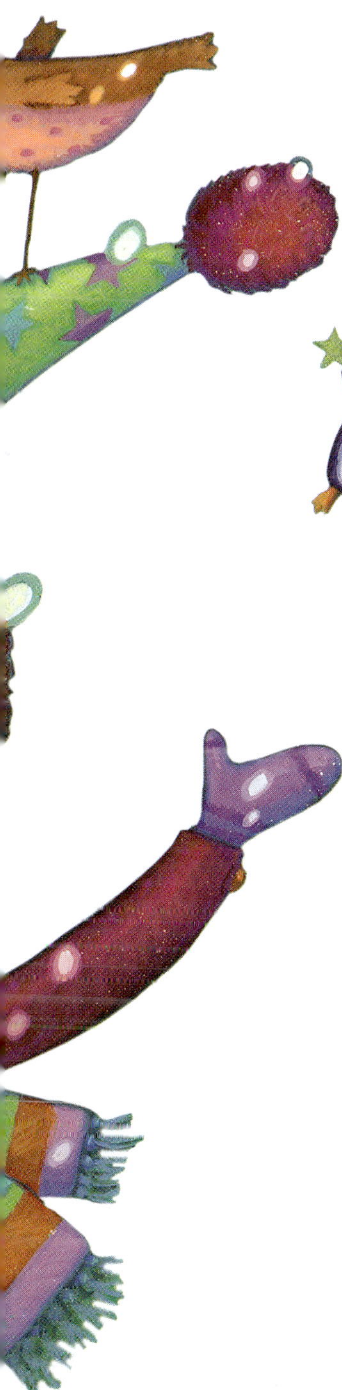

Marty Crisp
illustrated by Viv Eisner

SCHOLASTIC INC.
New York Toronto London Auckland Sydney
Mexico City New Delhi Hong Kong Buenos Aires

Originally published as *Totally Polar.*

ISBN 0-439-39128-8

12 11 10 9 8 7 6 5 4 3 2 2 3 4 5 6 7/0

Printed in the U.S.A. 14

First Scholastic printing, December 2002

The illustrations were rendered in gouache and colored pencil.
The text type was set in Lemonade ICG Bold.
The display type was set in Paisley ICG.
Designed by Lois A. Rainwater
Edited by Aimee Jackson

For Josh, who always likes it cold

—M.C.

To the sweet inspiration in my life, my daughter Anya,

and my pets, Cowboy Curtis, Weasel, and Blueberry

—V. E.

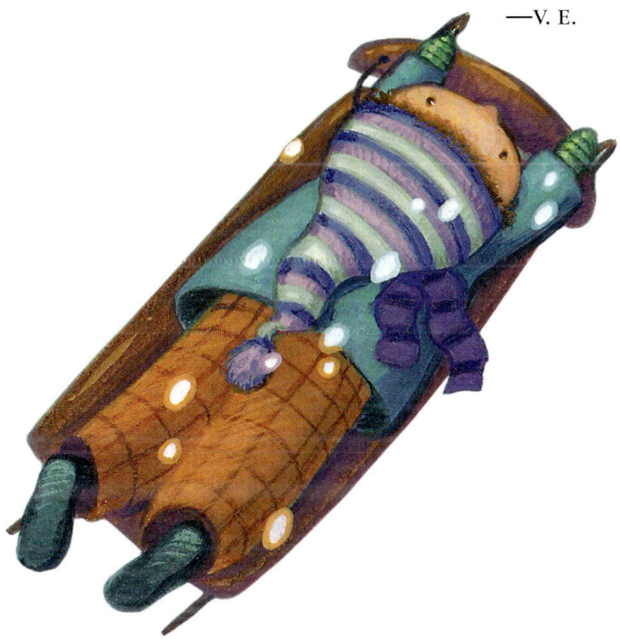

"Will it snow tomorrow,
and will there be school?"
asked Peter Petrosky
MacGregor O'Toole.

"Will it get
so deep
that it's up
to our door?"
asked Peter,
who lived
on the
23rd floor.

“So deep
that the reindeer
who fly Santa’s sleigh,
will have to
pull snowplows
to clear it away?”

"Will it get so cold
that it freezes my toes
and turns all my cats
into furry Eskimos?"

"In winter, you know,
lots of snow is the rule,"
said Peter Petrosky
MacGregor O'Toole.

"Then we'll build a snowman,
and roll him so tall
that we'll need a forklift
to place the last ball."

"We'll pour some
hot chocolate
and drink it in bed."

"And ride
to Alaska
and back
on my sled."

"As temperatures
drop, oh so fast
in the dark,
icebergs
will form
on the pond
in the park."

"Then we'll tear homework
from binders for fuel,"
said Peter Petrosky
MacGregor O'Toole.

"You're mad,"
said his mother,
"We're midway
through June,
and snow
is as likely
as cheese
on the moon.
So settle down nicely
and don't be a fool,
dear Peter Petrosky
MacGregor O'Toole."

His beach shoes are mukluks
(he thinks they look cool).
His swim trunks are long johns
and made out of wool.
When temperatures soar
and the world turns solar,
Peter Petrosky thinks only of polar.

If you see a boy
wearing mittens with shorts,
sailing white Arctic boats
into Popsicle ports,

who seems
to the season
to be a newcomer,
a boy of winter
who's stranded in summer,
a boy whose attitude
breaks every rule,
it's Peter
Petrosky
MacGregor
O'Toole.

MARTY CRISP's winter-loving son, Josh, was her inspiration for *Totally Polar*. Though the rest of the family likes the warmer months, Josh always prefers the cold.

Marty is the author of eleven published books, including seven books for children. Usually, she writes middle grade novels about dogs, like *Buzzard Breath, Private Captain,* and the 1999 Dog Writers Association of America Maxwell award winner, *Ratzo* (also by Rising Moon). Marty works as a reporter for the Lancaster Sunday News and lives in Lancaster County, Pennsylvania, with her husband, four kids, and three dogs.

VIV EISNER grew up in the snowy country of upstate New York. If she had lived on the 23rd floor, the snow would certainly have reached her door. As a child she loved color and was always painting or making something. In addition to painting, Viv also loves furry animals, reptiles, chocolate, melted cheese on anything, giggling, and singing loudly in her car.

Today Viv can still be found painting or making something in her Rhode Island home, where she lives with her daughter and several animals. This is her first picture book.